For the seeker in all of us – J.A.

Acknowledgements

Since I have no knowledge of Italian, I'm indebted to various translations, among them
Mark Musa's *A Portable Dante*; John Ciardi's *Divine Comedy* ; and Ciaran Carson's Irish-inflected *Inferno*.
My thanks also to Satoshi Kitamura for his awesome artwork; and of course to the man himself,
Dante Alighieri, for his monumental vision; and to Aesop for his treasury of fables.
Also, thanks to Frances Lincoln Publishers for their enthusiasm
along the *Young Inferno* road.

First published in Great Britain in 2008 and the USA in 2009 by
Frances Lincoln Children's Books, 4 Torriano Mews,
Torriano Avenue, London NW5 2RZ
www.franceslincoln.com

British Library Cataloguing in Publication Data
available on request

ISBN: 978-1-84507-769-3

Illustrated with black ink and watercolours

Set in Optima

Printed in Dongguan, Guangdong, China by South China Printing
9 8 7 6 5 4 3 2

THE YOUNG INFERNO

WRITTEN BY JOHN AGARD

ILLUSTRATED BY SATOSHI KITAMURA

F

FRANCES LINCOLN
CHILDREN'S BOOKS

Introduction

Some time after finishing *The Young Inferno*, I came across an internet article about Italian teenagers flocking to a Dante Disco Inferno. A DJ by the name of Alessio Bertallot and an actress called Lucilla Giagnoni teamed up to bring the 13th-century-born Florentine poet Dante Alighieri into nightclubs, where his verse was recited against a rock and techno soundscape. Yes, clubs and polytechnics were being transformed into Dantean circles of Hell, complete with spotlights and bodies caught in an apocalyptic techno-groove. An intriguing thought which might not have displeased the man himself, for in Dante's time many of his poems were sung.

Still, you've got to ask: why has Dante's *Inferno* inspired so many translations? It is the most translated poem in the Western tradition and has also inspired a movie trilogy, not to mention comic book style treatments, puppet shows, dance dramas, musical genres including classical and heavy metal – and, more recently, multi-media digital Dante. So what is it about this work, written over 700 years ago, that keeps on firing the imagination?

Let me say for starters, I don't speak Italian, and what you're about to read is in no way a translation. My only credentials are that I grew up a Roman Catholic and did my A-levels at a Jesuit College in Guyana. I have no regrets about an education that encouraged cricket as much as Latin and poetry, and you could say that even in the sunny Caribbean, we Roman Catholic boys had a fair notion of Hell.

But Dante's *Inferno* always seemed to me one of those formidable classics that you plan to read some good day but never get around to. Years later, when I did get around to it, our youngest daughter, Kalera, was in her teens, and she made sure the language and music of hip-hop permeated the air.

And it struck me that since Dante was interested in the everyday Italian heard in the street, and since teenagers are so wired to the world of horror movies, science fiction and video games, then they would feel quite at home with the virtual reality of Hell described by Dante with such magisterial and architectural precision. There you'll find your ascents and descents, your walkways and fortified gates, your spiralling levels not unlike a multi-storey car park.

For his tour guide to Hell, Dante uses the services of the Roman poet Virgil. For the tour guide of *The Young Inferno* I decided to use Aesop, whose fables Dante might have read in Latin translation and whose African ancestry is often forgotten (there's a suggestion that the name Aesop might have derived from *Aethiop* – 'Ethiopian'). I've also thrown in some notorious historical and political figures closer to our times. Here's hoping you can spot them under their disguise.

Since Dante built his three-part epic with such care for symmetry and the symbolic significance of numbers, I wanted to show some respect for these elements. The fact that the Italian word *stanza* has come to mean 'a room in a house' is a nice reminder of the architecture of Dante's work.

I have played around with the décor, but have kept those little rooms. And though *The Young Inferno* is told in 13 cantos (Dante's *Inferno* has 34), I hope that 13 sounds about right for a teenager and is in keeping with Dante's regard for the magic of numbers.

But if you're in a hurry to get to Hell, then skip this introduction. And here's hoping you meet your soulmate along the way. For we're all seekers, and behind this adventure into Hell lies a search for love.

John Agard

CANTO 1

In the middle of my childhood wonder
I woke to find myself in a forest
that was – how shall I put it – wild and sombre.

No sign of light. Not a star twinkling.
The whole thing was creepy and kind of crawly.
I still shudder in my trainers, just thinking

of those scary monsters lurking in the leaves,
and death itself putting on a grinning mask
and rehearsing its whispers for the breeze.

One moment I'm there, tidying my room.
Next moment, I'm listening to my heart leap
and nowhere to turn but tracks and tracks of gloom.

Maybe tomorrow I'll wake from this nightmare.
But right now this wilderness was for real.
Yes, I was swimming in a pool of fear.

I couldn't tell north from south, west from east.
Suddenly a leopard stood in front of me.
I screamed, 'Out of my way, you spotty beast!'

Now it was a lion that stared back at me,
shaking his golden mane with a great roar
and blocking my steps like a bully.

Next a she-wolf appeared, howling for blood.
The air trembled with the sound, and I thought,
Why me? Do I look like Red Riding Hood?

I wondered what these three creatures could mean.
A leopard. A lion. A she-wolf –
all scary to look at, yet somehow serene.

Then a dark man appeared over a tree-top.
No taller than a dwarf, he spoke from high.
'I'm your guide,' he said. 'My name is Aesop.'

'Spot on, my son. Memory will serve you well
as we continue on our journey –
which, by the way, leads to the depths of Hell.

So better start tuning up your ears
for the shrieks and groans of all those
who sizzle in the flames of their own tears.

My job is to see you get there safely.
But you'll have to go by another road.
Then I'll leave you to the Good Fairy.'

So my guide, Aesop, walked on. I followed close.

CANTO 2

If only I'd charged my mobile phone
I could have texted my parents there and then:
Off 2 Hell with teacher Aesop. Not alone.

And as we took each slope in heavy stride
he told me stories to lift my spirits.
I'd say he was an entertaining guide.

'Once there was this wolf that got into trouble
when a dreaded lamb's bone stuck in his throat.
Heron came to Wolf's side on the double.

As it happened, Wolf had promised a fee
to whosoever removed the bone
and put him out of his agony.

Down Wolf's throat went Heron's surgeon beak.
And after a professional probe
out came the bone, much to Wolf's relief.

"My fee," said Heron. "We had an arrangement."
Wolf grinned. "What fee? What if I had closed my jaws?
I spared your neck and that's enough payment."

Ingratitude wears both beast and human mask.'
At that point I raised my hand politely.
'Please, sir, I have a question to ask:

Shouldn't the heron have done that kind deed
without thought of payment or reward?
Doesn't the Wolf deserve to be pitied?'

My teacher said, 'You've got a point. Quite right.
It just shows that neither beast nor man
can be divided into black and white.

But all will be made clear when we go below.
It's not far now to the gates of Hell.
Soon you'll meet the Good Fairy, your shadow.

She'll guide you back to that shining hill –
the one you strayed from when those three beasts
stopped you in your tracks. Now, have you the will?'

'You are my guide,' I said. 'I'm following you.'

When I saw these words above a gate
I felt a sad and weird sensation.
'Can we turn back?' I said. 'Is it too late?'

My teacher smiled and said, 'This is Hell, my son.
What do you expect? A red carpet
and bunches of flowers that say *Welcome*?'

Then, holding my hand, he whispered to me,
'Nothing is more fearsome than your fear.
Just think of Hell as a scary movie.'

And with these words of encouragement
he led me down starless winding stairs.
I could hear voices coming from a basement.

There was every accent you could imagine –
howls of pain uttered in every language.
I asked my teacher, 'Why all this wailing?'

'These are the people who sat on the fence.
They cared neither for good nor for evil.
Theirs was the sin of indifference.

Think back to the time the birds and animals
called for an election to decide which one
should be sacrificed to the gods in ritual.

"I'm not bothered," said Fowl-Cock. "I'm easy.
I never attend any boring meetings.
As long as I can crow, the world's fine by me."

In his absence, the others cast their vote.
And unanimously they agreed to give
the sacrificial chop to Fowl-Cock's throat.'

'That's not fair,' I exclaimed. 'I can't bear their cries.'
'Well, my boy, you'd be screaming like these poor souls
if your skin was covered with wasps and flies.

'Save your tears,' he said, 'for we must pass on
across murky waters to that other shore.
Here he comes, the old ferryman Charon.'

Charon cried, 'I am the ferryman of death.
I ferry only the tormented dead.
I'll have no boy aboard with living breath.'

It was good to hear the ferryman's words.
They reassured me that I was still alive
though I had crossed the Otherworld.

Then the ferryman prodded the souls aboard.
'Get a move on,' said flame-eyed Charon.
All who lingered got a whack from his oar.

I gazed at the white waterfall of his beard
as he pushed off with his weeping boatload
and drifted into the darkening air.

I pinched myself and surrendered to sleep...

CANTO 4

And so we crossed from Hell's First Circle
into the Second, with less space than the First.
And the groans were worse, if that's possible.

I felt a chilly finger down my spine.
There, standing like a bouncer at the entrance
was none other than one called Frankenstein.

He was frisking souls for scandalous traces
and looked like a man who enjoyed his job –
directing the dead to their reserved places.

'O heart of man and monster twinned as one!'
(This is how Aesop addressed Frankenstein.)
'What's the reason for these souls' damnation?'

'Here is where the lovesick come to suffer twice.'
Frankenstein scowled as he said these words.
'I too have known what loneliness feels like. Ice.

In the still hours, how I longed for a mate.
Was a wife and kids too much to ask for?
Never thought I'd end up keeper of Hell's gate.'

Turning to my teacher, Frankenstein said,
'Why bring a boy here? You should know better.
What does he know of love? Besides, he ain't dead.'

'It is good that the lad should see for himself
how love still shoots its burning arrows
into souls that lived their lives all for the flesh...'

My teacher winked at me kindly as he spoke.
'These days the young have old heads on their shoulders.
They've seen it all in magazines and soaps.'

He showed me souls flapping wildly in a wind.
'Where are their beautiful bodies now?' he asked.
'Look how the whirlwind batters them like starlings.

There's strong Samson weeping for his Delilah.
There's Cleopatra gutted for her Anthony –
and still going like moths to love's sweet fire.'

Frankenstein grinned: 'Love's not a bad way to burn.
And if it's scandal you want, this is the place.
Don't look so shocked, boy. Just feast your eyes and learn.

Take that baby-faced Tristan, for example –
he had the hots for a queen named Isolde –
but guess what? She was the wife of his uncle.'

'All right, Frankenstein, no need to go on.
That's enough sex education for one day.
I see Hell's Third Circle on the horizon.'

'Maybe you'll find a girlfriend there, who knows?'
Frankenstein grinned at his own joke and started
singing, as he sorted out souls and shadows:

'I've heard love flutter its turtledove wings.
I've seen love look back at me with puppy eyes.
Oh, love makes a grunting monster want to sing.'

His song made me think of Beauty and the Beast.
My teacher said, 'Love can make you do strange things.
Like the lion that fell head-over-heels

in love with a drop-dead gorgeous maiden.
When the lion proposed marriage, her parents
of course were gob-smacked. "That's a bit sudden."

Not wanting to offend the jungle King
they suggested he remove his fangs and claws.
Then they'd gladly discuss the wedding ring.

Teeth out, claws trimmed, Lion came back to impress.
But the parents laughed in his face. "Buzz off, sunshine."
Which goes to show how love can tame the wildest.'

Frankenstein was still singing when we left.

CANTO 5

When I woke up, no light was visible.
Thunder sounded in my ears until I heard
my teacher say, 'Nearly there. Hell's Third Circle.'

Around its brink lay a bottomless abyss
of screaming faces from every nation.
(Never know who you'll meet in a place like this.)

It was like being at a Halloween party
except that the screams were not pretend.
How could they keep this up for eternity?

Even my good teacher's face had grown pale.
'You go first,' I said. 'If you are frightened,
what about me? Without you, I'll surely fail.'

'It's not fear, but pity that's changed my colour.
I feel sorry for these sighing souls.
And I recognise many a dead scholar.

See where that beam of light rings the dark?
Have a good look. Would you believe that lot
once shone in the sciences and arts?

'There's Euclid, mathematical legend,
now a victim of his own geometry,
condemned to draw a straight line without end.

There's blind Homer, brandishing a sword
like one of his Greek heroes – a poet doomed
to recite his epics backwards, word for word.

There's old Archimedes, still running a bath.
What principle does he hope to discover
in a place where the dark is your only path?

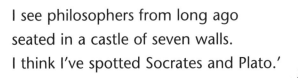

I see philosophers from long ago
seated in a castle of seven walls.
I think I've spotted Socrates and Plato.'

My teacher seemed to know everyone there.
The only one I knew was brainy Einstein.
You couldn't miss that mane of shock-white hair.

I'd read somewhere that Einstein's theory
provided the key to the atom bomb.
But why was he here? Didn't seem fair to me.

'Your Einstein has a bright and kindly face.
But theories, you know, can get out of hand
when they're in the hands of the human race.

How was he to know that his equation
would lead to two cities' devastation?
All the more reason to cherish reason.

Like the time humans first stood before God
and began to moan about their condition
(as if whingeing and whining did any good):

"You've given the birds wings, the cheetah speed.
You've given the fish scales, the lion strength.
What have you done for us in our naked need?"

God replied: "Stronger than strong, swifter than swift –
such is reason which I've given you.
Will you make a curse or blessing of my gift?"'

My teacher said no more in that spooky wind

CANTO 6

Standing guard and staring straight at me
was an oversized Rottweiler with three heads.
I forget his name, but it wasn't Lassie.

Since his three mouths were yapping all at once –
and his fangs, I tell you, weren't a pretty sight –
I paused. But there was no other entrance.

Here bloated souls emitted foul breezes.
Gluttony had brought them to Hell's Third Circle.
They were up to their necks in beans and cheeses.

My teacher sighed and said, 'Bet that lot
never spared a thought for the starving.
But my mother always said, "Waste not, want not."

Though these folks are no longer flesh and blood,
see for yourself, son, look how sluggishly they move,
still weighed down by thoughts of material goods.

The world's divided, by my reckoning,
into the overfed and the underfed.
Famine goes hand in hand with food mountains.

There's that emperor Heliogabalus,
who loved novelties like lentils in onyx.
Even dead, his taste buds are notorious.

There's a Tudor king tucking into second course:
boiled mutton, swan, roast boar with pudding.
Hell's Third Circle must seem like Hampton Court.'

Fancy stuffing one's face for eternity,
I thought, as I watched cardinals choking on
never-ending serpents of spaghetti.

I saw one emperor of old who knocked back
500 figs, 400 oysters and more,
all at one sitting. What a digestive tract!

I saw modern souls licking canapés
that left them all the more ravenous.
They howled at the sight of each passing tray.

And the smells! No, not a place to hang around.
The rain was pelting down. And as for the hail,
it was like a swarm of wasps. It really stung.

My teacher fed the yapping beast some mud and said, 'Hush!
One lump of mud down each of your three throats.'
Then we took a path of what looked like gold-dust.

My teacher said, 'Every feast must come to an end.'

CANTO 7

At the door we met Mammon, the money god,
strutting around in his glittering bling-bling –
and still wearing flares. I thought, what a vain sod.

'Welcome to Hell's Fourth Circle,' smirked Mammon.
'Money talks, so excuse the clinks and rustling.
That's just money having a conversation.'

Between his lips a gold-tipped cigarette-holder
competed with the gold between his teeth. He said,
'Here you'll find souls who lived for the dollar.

We've had some famous customers here below:
Cortés, Columbus, Raleigh, the odd stockbroker,
still searching for their golden El Dorado.'

I saw souls sucked into fruit machines
which spat them back out in a gush of coins
that never stopped. And there was no end of screams.

The place went berserk when two rival gangs clashed:
the Big-Spenders versus the Tight-Fisters.
And all their bickering was over cash.

'Wasters!' screamed one gang. 'Misers!' screamed the other.
Even their shadows argued and came to blows.
'What about words like *sister* and *brother*?'

asked my teacher. 'Shouldn't money be shared
fairly and put to good use? Why hoard it?
Like that miser, you know, who lived in fear

of thieves running off with the lump of gold
he'd buried at the bottom of his garden.
One night, thieves did just that – broke in and stole

the treasured lump that cost him so much sleep.
When the neighbours heard the news, they consoled him.
"Don't bother, old man, don't bother to weep.

All you did was hoard and admire the gold.
You never spread any joy with it. Why not
admire a stone in the hole, silly old goat?"'

'But, Teacher,' I said, 'Should we jump to conclusions?
The old geezer, I agree, was a skinflint.
But that lump might have been for his pension.'

'Boy, don't you start talking economics,'
my teacher said. 'Time to leave these greedy souls
and cross the slimy waters of the river Styx.'

And so I followed my teacher's cherished footsteps.

CANTO 8

Two small flames flickered from a high tower.
What we thought a candle, must be a signal.
Someone flashed a torch and was coming closer.

Then a boat skimmed the bog in a split second.
'What's the meaning of this?' I asked my teacher.
'It's the old barge-lady. Beware her sharp tongue.

She can be as ugly as your worst nightmare.
She can be as beautiful as you wish.
Rumour has it she's skilled at changing shape.

Only the dead will discover her true name.
But to the living she is simply Crone,
and this part of the Styx is her domain.'

'You!' she said, pointing at me with her barge-pole.
'Buzz off! Find your way back to the living.
But I'll have your teacher. Hop on, dead soul.'

'O sweet Crone, who speaks with voice of oracle,'
said my teacher, choosing his words with care,
'grant the boy entry into Hell's Sixth Circle.

We're not that far now from the city of Dis.
It is willed that he should make this journey.
He couldn't retrace his footsteps, if he wished.'

I should have done like Hansel and Gretel –
dropped a trail of stones to mark my way.
But get real, man, we're talking about Hell.

There was no way I'd dream of going alone.
'Good Teacher, 'I said, 'please stay with me.'
Then I heard these pleasing words of Crone:

'Your teacher speaks well, so I'll grant this favour.
I'll take you two as far as the far shore.
But no photos allowed in Dis, remember.'

I thought Crone's sense of humour kind of grim.
The last thought on our minds as we journeyed
was to capture the experience on film.

So I joked that I'd heard of the city Dis,
where everybody disses everybody.
'Enjoy yourselves,' said Crone. 'But expect no bliss.'

We thanked her and made for the city gate.
Stroppy angels threw stones to stop us –
in fact, they slammed the gate in my teacher's face.

I could see he was taken by surprise.
It scared me to see my teacher grow pale.
'Never mind,' he said. 'Fortune's help will arrive.'

I had faith in my teacher, a man of his word.
All I said was, 'Fortune's help? But when?'
Then my questions, like my prayers, were answered.

Out of the blue-dark, up comes a godly wind
and sweeps the gate loose from its hinges,
wide enough to let me and my teacher in.

My teacher said, 'Fortune comes to a smiling gate.'

CANTO 9

Definitely not your average city, Dis:
tall iron buildings with tall iron stairs –
in short, a cold, iron metropolis.

A gang of snake-haired women in T-shirts
saying FURIES looked set to mug us.
'Get that one! He looks fresh-faced from Earth.'

They called for back-up from their mate Gorgon
to turn the likes of me into stone.
Yet Aesop addressed them as 'Good Ones',

for he had met them before and knew their ways.
'Whatever you do, boy, don't look!'
And he shielded my eyes from Gorgon's gaze.

He protested that we'd committed no crime.
It was willed that we should visit Dis.
And Fortune's winds came to save us in time.

A storm swept the gang down streets lined with tombs
which just so happened to be half-open.
I dared not look inside to see who was who.

'Those tombs, good lad, belong to the heretics
who say that when the body dies, the soul dies.
Come Judgment Day, they'll close with a final click.

There's more to Dis than meets the eye, my son.
Within these walls are circles within
circles – each one a different kind of prison.

You'll find fraudsters who conned old-age pensioners.
Here's where they end up, like those who do
violence to themselves and to their neighbours.'

'But, Teacher, why is that soul being whirled around
on a wheel that is forever spinning?
What crime brought him to Hell's kingdom?'

'He caused a child's death in a stolen car.
But did he stop? No. And that's because
he had drunk himself over the limit by far.

But, my boy, we'd better get a move on.
We've seen enough of Hell's Sixth Circle.
Who knows what's waiting on the horizon?'

I followed him without any hesitation.

CANTO 10

We went down the slope to Hell's Seventh Circle,
and didn't expect a bull-headed man
to present us with another obstacle.

'Be off!' said my teacher. 'Get lost, Minotaur.
Who do you think you are, standing there
like some sort of immigration officer?'

The beast went off, feeding on his own rage.
But suddenly I saw other beasts,
this time half-horse, half-man – and on the rampage.

'Good day to you, sir,' said my teacher to one
who was obviously the leader.
And that's when I met the Centaur Chiron.

Chiron seemed to me a nice enough bloke
despite his hooves and flaring nostrils.
He patted my arm and attempted a joke.

'Is this living flesh?' he said in wonder.
'Because if you're not dead, my young friend,
I presume you're down here as an observer.

And since you ain't got wings, just an earthbound kid.
I'll lend you Nessus, a fellow Centaur,
to fly you around the crimes humankind did.'

With my teacher moving lighter than a dance
and a Centaur's shoulders for my saddle,
we flew through souls now boiling in their conscience.

'There's that King who slaughtered the innocents.
Even his crown of gold keeps hissing
as he cries out his twitches and torments.

There's that Inquisitor, there's that Goose-stepper.
Don't they deserve each other? Well, you know what
they say – birds of a feather flock together.

There's that smooth duo who caused much blood to flow
between the Tigris and Euphrates.
But leaders, like new world orders, come and go.

I'll call no names, that's not my intention.
But they'll see themselves in history's mirror,
if they can bear the sight of their own reflection.'

'But can we learn anything from animals?'
I asked my well-informed half-horse, half-man.
'Ask your teacher, Aesop. He's fable-full.'

'What can humans learn?' Aesop said. 'Mercy.
And maybe a sense of gratitude.
Or even how the small might help the mighty.

Lion was in his den having a sound sleep
when a nosey mouse ran across his nose.
"Who's that come to disturb my royal dreams?"

Lion growled, as he raised a lethal paw.
"So sorry, Your Majesty," replied the mouse,
"but I meant no harm. I'll never break your law."

"But you break my sleep!" The King of Beasts frowned.
"Give one reason why I should let you go."
Mouse said, "I may rescue you some day you're down."

Lion never laughed so much in his life.
"You? Rescue me? Run along, you little squirt."
Later, Lion shared the joke with his wife.

But Lion didn't laugh when the hunters' net
bound him hand and foot in sudden rope.
Nothing Lion could do but accept death.

His groans reached every ear in the forest
and the mouse came running without delay.
"I'm not the kind who forgets a kindness.

Remember, once you spared my life, Your Majesty.
Now it's Mouse to the rescue. Stay still.
My teeth will do the job and set you free."'

This story cheered us on to Hell's Eighth Circle.

CANTO 11

Dear Reader, you haven't heard the half of it.
Getting through the Seventh Circle took
some doing, I tell you. Yes, it took some grit.

I thought no way we'd come out of there alive –
the raining fire... the burning snow...
the sucking sands... Yet we managed to survive

with a little help from friends in high places.
Like that Centaur who gave me a ride.
Like that Crone who rowed us across the Styx.

Now I'm on the brink of Hell's Eighth Circle –
ring within ring, a sloping theatre.
To work out directions makes the mind boggle.

At times like this you really need a map.
My teacher said, 'We'll follow our nose.
Take a right. Ignore those demons at our back.'

So we passed the malicious and the vicious
up to their eyelashes in a ditch,
and they screamed at us every possible curse:

'Pimple-Face! Get back to where you came from!
We don't want no foreigners from Earth!
If you ain't dead, then you just ain't welcome!'

I never knew the dead held such prejudices
against the living. 'Teacher, what's this place?'
'This is Malborge, Place of the Evil Ditches.'

Then it dawned on me that ditch led into ditch
like a series of moats round a castle.
I couldn't tell the entrance from the exit.

To reach each ditch you had to cross a stone dyke
(the architect had thought of everything)
perfect for skateboarding or a mountain bike –

that's if you see yourself as a daredevil
and as long as you're not allergic
to beasties following you at every level.

I heard voices crying from inside thorn trees
where weird birds with wise-woman faces
stood guard. 'Teacher, explain those voices, please.'

'They are those, my son, who wounded Mother Earth.
They plundered her heart, uprooted her lungs.
Now thorn-pricks are giving them their money's worth.

As for those birds with the old-lady expression,
don't be fooled. They're disguised wind-goddesses,
here to teach those exploiters a lesson.'

'All right, we admit we made Earth's green a dump,'
screamed the souls inside those stunted trees.
'But do we deserve pitchforks in our rump?'

Their screams followed us as we passed jagged rocks
and I saw souls with heads facing backwards –
so when they wept, their tears ran down their buttocks.

'Those are your spin-doctors who fiddle the future,'
my teacher explained. 'They live on hindsight.
Facing the past is their outstanding feature.'

'And who's the one dragging her feet among the dead?'
'Oh, that one used to be a high-flyer
but now her golden shoes are filled with lead.'

At the fifth ditch the bridge began to bend.
A voice said, 'Can I be of assistance?
I'm Evil-Tail, Chief Devil here, and your friend.

As you can see, I'm neither black nor white.
Some see the he in me, some see the she.
One of these days I must set the record right.

Yes, I know the Devil gets a bad press.
But forget all those things the tabloids said.
Look, trust me. I'm at your service. Be my guests.'

My teacher said, 'The world knows your tongue is forked.
But we'd like to take up your kind offer.
Will you really guide us, or is it just talk?'

He grinned. 'Evil-Tail does as Evil-Tail speaks.'
Then he pointed to some prancing demons.
'This happy bunch are my assistants, not freaks.

There's Bugle-Bum, there's Running-Belly. Come on,
smile for our young visitor from Earth.'
Bugle-Bum exploded, to bid me welcome.

So with this lot for our bodyguards, we came
to a ditch, where they chose to leave us stranded.
'Promise-breakers!' shouted my teacher. 'What's your game?'

He shook his head. 'See, my son, they can't be trusted.'
The demons giggled: 'It's departure lounge.
Have a good trip. And may your flesh be gutted!'

'It's down to us, son. We'll go it on our own.
Chin up. Mind you don't step over those tusks.
This must be the Valley of Endangered Bones.

Now, let me get my bearings right. If that's the exit,
then we're at the entrance to the sixth ditch.
I see wolves in sheep's clothing. The hypocrites!

See that frying friar? Well, here are some facts.
That same missionary who preached goodness
tortured Mayan Indians with burning wax.'

'Teacher, tell me, are there many more ditches?
I've seen plunderers, hypocrites, torturers...
I can't take much more of bastards and bitches.'

'Son, we've still to come to the ditch of liars.
You'll find them among the movers and shakers
from all races. Mischief-making falsifiers!'

Teacher,' I joked, 'Mind if we wait for a bus?'
'My boy, you've still got your sense of humour.
But I think I see Hell's Ninth Circle before us.'

So goodbye, Malborge, Place of the Evil Ditches.

CANTO 12

Here we were – Hell's Ninth Circle, at long last.
We came to the edge of a frozen lake
and crocodiles saluted as we passed.

'Bet you've never seen crocodiles with medals!'
my teacher said, managing a smile.
'That lot still think they're lieutenant-generals.

There's that one whose name rhymes with empire.
When faced with a group of unarmed pilgrims
he commanded his troops to open fire.

There's that one who shot a village in Vietnam.
He's still splashing his tail on the trigger
and swears God's on the side of Uncle Sam.'

'But Teacher,' I said. 'that's not fair to reptiles.
For crocs may have fangs, crocs may have scales, but crocs
aren't human enough for guns and missiles.'

'Well said, son. A croc may be a predator,
but I've yet to meet a croc in a moustache
or a croc that grew into a dictator.

White, black or yellow, they all have one view.
With moustaches or without moustaches,
over killing fields they'll raise their own statue.

Like that one there in the goose-stepping boots.
Though frozen, he's convinced he's a master croc.
That's why he bows to himself and salutes.

'Or that Caucasian son of a shoemaker –
wouldn't his skin do for a handbag or shoe?
May the voices he silenced purge his liver!

And see that croc there with the field-marshal grin?
Bet he'd prefer to bask in African sun
than to freeze on this lake for the sake of sin.

Crocodile skin is now their new uniform,'
my teacher explained. 'But these wretched souls
might well improve if they changed to a worm.

See, for instance, that multitude of maggots?
Don't be fooled, boy. They were once the heartless
tyrants who trod on the hearts of the have-nots.

And see that log where those toads are making plans?
Listen well, and you'll hear them discussing
what's called Man's inhumanity to Man.'

Then one toad turned to me a sad-looking face.
'Get me out!' he cried. 'There's been a mistake.
I shouldn't have been here in the first place.

History knows me as Attila the Hun
who ravaged countless cities in the Balkans.
But deep down, I'm still a family man.

Why am I here among this croaking mob?
Somebody somewhere must have stitched me up.
I never once touched a nuclear bomb.'

'That's enough,' my teacher said to Attila.
'Don't burden the boy with your excuses.
I know we can't all be Nelson Mandela.

But whatever your race, your shape or your -ism,
I've got news for warmongers and tyrants:
Hell's Ninth Circle will be your five-star prison.'

And so we passed the Lake of the Frozen Crocs,
down through the Valley of the Teeming Toads
till we came to the Ridge of the Weeping Rocks.

Here my teacher stopped and gave me an embrace.
'Come, my son. Don't say a word. Just listen...
to the sound of Death weeping for the human race.

But, despite everything, who'd want to let go
the joy of waking to a new morning
and come to one of Hell's circles below?

There was once an old man who'd had enough –
enough of problems, I mean – debts and all that.
'O Death, come take my load," he said once, in a huff.

Death happened to be passing by, and stopped.
"Can I be of some assistance?" Death asked.
I'm not ready for death – not by my clock!

thought the old man, who was fetching firewood.
"Sorry to trouble you, Death. All I meant was:
help me lift this wood. Ah, Death, you're so good."

'And now, my boy, you too must follow your bliss.
Here is where we go our separate ways.
But you're bound to meet someone across that abyss.'

'Dear teacher,' I cried, 'come with me to the Upper World.'
'No, my son, my place is in the Lower.
And your fortune may be in the form of a girl.'

He winked, and said as we parted, 'The Good Fairy.'

CANTO 13

Back in the Upper World of familiar faces
I didn't expect to see a vision –
not in the library, of all places.

I saw her lost to the world in a book,
and my mind turned the pages of her hair.
How can I forget that otherworldly look?

I could have said, 'That book, is it scary?'
or something like, 'Have you got the time?'
Instead, I mumbled, 'Are you the good fairy?'

I felt stupid just asking the question.
Luckily she said, 'No, my name isn't Mary.'
Even sitting, she was poetry in motion.

I remember the time our eyes made first glimpse.
Yes, it was precisely nine o'clock.
My pulse leapt to the sound of her name: Beatrice.

'But all my friends just call me B,' she said.
I should have said B for Blessed, B for Beauty.
I knew then, her voice would be music to my head.

Oh, how I was lost in the orbit of Beatrice.
Was she for real, or some otherworldly
vision from a daydreamer's kind of mist?

In the blinding light, she's the soothing dark.
In the dreaming dark, she's the hidden light.
She's the shadow who guides my inner spark.

I danced in the chemistry of her eyes
and I could have chilled out there for ever.
She made that library a paradise.

Yes, that May Day meeting began my own spring.